"Here you are, John," Ulka said, offering him a fat grub, whose many legs were wiggling in a frenzy to get away.

John Midas stared at it in horror and made no attempt to take the squirming creature from her. "You expect me to *eat* it?" he said. "Don't you think this—this thing—would be better cooked, Bam?"

" 'Cooked'?" Bam said.

John felt very sorry for him. "Would you like me to try cooking a couple? I can grill them over a fire," he said.

" 'Fire'?" he said. "What's that?"

John laughed. Bam must be kidding.

"Seriously. Where's the fireplace?" John asked.

But there was no fireplace, and no fire.

John realized that if he wanted to eat cooked grubs, then he would have to show them how to make a fire!

JOHN MIDAS IN THE DREAMTIME
a new John Midas adventure from
the author of THE CHOCOLATE TOUCH

JOHN MIDAS
IN THE
DREAMTIME

PATRICK SKENE CATLING
ILLUSTRATED BY JEAN JENKINS LOEWER

A BANTAM SKYLARK BOOK®
TORONTO • NEW YORK • LONDON • SYDNEY • AUCKLAND

RL 4, 008-012

*This low-priced Bantam Book
has been completely reset in a typeface
designed for easy reading, and was printed
from new plates. It contains the complete
text of the original hardcover edition.*
NOT ONE WORD HAS BEEN OMITTED.

JOHN MIDAS IN THE DREAMTIME

*A Bantam Skylark Book / published by arrangement with
William Morrow and Company, Inc.*

PRINTING HISTORY
William Morrow edition published October 1986

*Skylark Books is a registered trademark of Bantam Books, Inc.
Registered in U.S. Patent and Trademark Office and elsewhere.*

Bantam Skylark edition / December 1987

Bantam Books are published by Bantam Books, Inc. Its trademark, consisting of the words "Bantam Books" and the por-
trayal of a rooster, is Registered in U.S. Patent and Trademark
Office and in other countries. Marca Registrada. Bantam
Books, Inc., 666 Fifth Avenue, New York, New York 10103.

PRINTED IN THE UNITED STATES OF AMERICA

S   0 9 8 7 6 5 4 3 2 1

For Alys

1

John Midas was at home with a cold the day his class studied Australia. He did not know much about the country, but he was glad when his father said the family would go there for their Christmas vacation. It would be a change. They usually stayed at home at that time of the year, and had to clear away a lot of snow.

At breakfast one Sunday morning a few

days before the end of school, Mr. Midas told them about the trip. "I have to go to a meeting in Canberra for a few days," he said. "It's the capital of Australia. Then we can go wherever we like."

"We'll go to Sydney, the biggest city, of course," Mrs. Midas said with a happy smile. "The Opera House, the art galleries, the museums!"

"Is there a ballet?" asked John's young sister, Mary, who had started taking dancing lessons and could already balance on the tips of her toes without wobbling much.

"Probably," John muttered without enthusiasm. His mother's and sister's ideas of fun sometimes seemed more like school projects.

"They say Sydney Harbour's great for sailing," Mr. Midas said. "Everybody has a sailboat."

"That won't do us much good at Christmastime, will it?" John asked.

"Christmastime's the Australian summer," Mary replied. She was younger than John but she read more books.

"How can it be?" he asked.

"Australia's on the other side of the world," Mr. Midas explained. "When we're farthest away from the sun, they're nearest. So our summer's their winter."

"Oh, sure," John said, nodding, pretending to understand. Mary recognized his blank expression and gave him one of her teasing grins. When she tried, she could be very annoying.

"The world's the shape of an orange, you see," she said. "Or hasn't Miss Plimsole gotten around to teaching you that yet?"

"Now, children!" Mrs. Midas interrupted.

"Australia's huge," Mary said. "It's as big as . . . as Alaska!"

"A lot bigger," Mr. Midas said. "It's almost as big as the United States."

"Will we go sailing?" John asked.

"We'll see," Mrs. Midas said. This usually meant "No."

"We'll sail across the harbor in one of those hydrofoil sightseeing boats," Mr. Midas promised. "You'll like it, John. They're very fast."

"We won't have time for sailboats," Mrs. Midas said. "We can go sailing any summer, here on the lake. We're going to make the most of every day in Australia. We'll do things we can't do here—Australian things. We'll go to Ayers Rock, near Alice Springs."

"Where's *that*?" John asked.

Even his clever little sister did not know.

Mr. Midas went and got the atlas. They looked at a map of the world and found Australia easily enough, a great island at the bottom of the right-hand side, down at the far edge of the Pacific Ocean. Then they looked at a map of Australia. It took a

bit longer to find Alice Springs. It was just a small dot in a big, empty space, almost exactly in the middle of the country.

"It's about as far away from everything as you could possibly go," Mr. Midas said.

"It's the most Australian part of Australia," Mrs. Midas added. "The heart of the Outback! Ayers Rock is unique. They say it's the oldest mountain in the oldest part of the oldest land on Earth. Visiting Ayers Rock will be a very educational experience."

"Who says?" John asked.

"The books in the library. They say the original natives of Australia have always believed that Ayers Rock is . . . well, *magic*."

Leaning close to the atlas, John thought of pirates examining the map of "Treasure Island" and he felt the small hairs at the back of his neck prickle with excitement.

2

While Mr. Midas attended to his business
in Canberra, Mrs. Midas kept John and
Mary busy sightseeing. She took them on
a guided tour around Lake Burley Griffin,
which was named after the man who designed the capital city, and showed them
the Captain Cook Memorial Water Jet, a
fountain that spurts 140 feet up in the air;
the Royal Australian Mint, a factory where
Australian money is manufactured; and

Parliament House, where legislators make the country's laws.

"Is there going to be a quiz?" John asked with a yawn.

"Don't be sarcastic," Mrs. Midas said.

"We're very lucky, seeing all these important buildings, aren't we?" Mary said in her politest school voice.

Sydney was another blur of guided touring. They saw Sydney Harbour Bridge, the Opera House, the Sydney Tower at Centrepoint, the Royal Botanic Gardens, and the Art Gallery of New South Wales.

"Did you have fun, you guys?" Mr. Midas asked, when the family got together again.

"It was *very* interesting," Mary said.

John only raised his eyebrows and sighed.

But soon the Midas family was aboard a plane bound for Alice Springs, and John's hopes revived.

When the plane reached its cruising altitude, about five miles above the ground, the passengers were allowed to unfasten their seat belts. The flight crew began to serve drinks from a cart, which they pushed along the aisle between the rows of seats. John asked for a soda, but Mary had a much cleverer idea.

"Please may I go to the front and say 'hello' to the pilots?" she asked a stewardess. When Mary very much wanted something, she had a way of opening her blue eyes especially wide. John had often noticed that when she did so, strangers usually gave her anything she wanted. More than one person had commented that she looked like "a little angel"—a notion that gave him a pain in the stomach.

"As soon as I finish serving drinks, I'll ask the captain," the stewardess replied with a sweet, encouraging smile. A little later, she returned to Mary's seat and said, "The captain says you can come forward to the flight deck now."

"Can I come, too?" John asked.

"I'm sorry," the stewardess said. "Only one. Maybe another time."

The stewardess opened the door at the top of the aisle for Mary and closed it behind her. John remained in his seat, biting his lower lip with envy. He wondered why little sisters had all the luck.

Mary was away for what seemed to John to be a long time. When she came back, she was beaming.

"It was lovely," she said.

John said nothing.

"The captain let me sit in the seat beside him," she added. "He let me steer the plane. Did you know that planes have two steering wheels?"

"Of course I did," John said. He realized you are not supposed to hate your own sister, but at moments like this she made it difficult for him not to. Fortunately, the flight soon came to an end, so he was able to think of other things.

It was a hot, dry December afternoon, and when the plane taxied from the end of the runway to the passenger terminal at Alice Springs, the engines blew up clouds of dust.

"Funny weather for Christmas," John said, as they walked down the steps from the plane.

"Sometimes it's even hotter than this," Mr. Midas told him.

"We'll go back with fabulous tans," Mary said in a cheery voice. "All my friends will be jealous."

"We must get some lotion," Mrs. Midas said anxiously.

A taxi took them to their hotel. It was a new one, in an oasis of green grass and palm trees. There were red tennis courts and a blue swimming pool. In the cool lobby, a sign showed the way to *The Casino*. The bedrooms were pale beige, furnished with enormous beds.

"It's like Las Vegas," Mary said, who had seen Las Vegas on television at home.

"Hotels are all the same," said Mrs. Midas. "We aren't staying here long, so as soon as we're organized, we're going to see the *real* Australia. Aren't we, dear?" she asked Mr. Midas.

Mr. Midas nodded in agreement. Then he telephoned and arranged to rent a Range Rover, with fat tires, which are good for driving over rough roads.

"Make sure there are two good spares," he said, "a shovel in case we get stuck in the desert sand, and cans full of extra gasoline and drinking water." He hung up the phone. "This will be an adventure!" he exclaimed.

"Now," Mrs. Midas said in a serious voice, "I want you kids to have a rest. It has been a long day. Daddy and I have some shopping to do." John and Mary began to groan in protest about being left behind, but their mother held up a hand to silence them. "You can watch television. We'll be back soon. Then we'll all go down to the dining room for an early dinner. You can see Alice Springs in the morning, before we leave for Ayers Rock."

Mary secretly winked at John, so he knew she had an idea and he did not say anything.

As soon as Mr. and Mrs. Midas had left, Mary picked up the telephone and asked for room service. She gave their room number and said, "We want two banana splits with everything on them—chocolate, vanilla, and strawberry ice cream, crushed pineapple, caramel, and whipped cream."

When she paused for a moment to think, John added, "And cherries on top."

"And cherries on top," she agreed.

While they waited, they rolled around on the king-size beds, triumphantly giggling.

In the hotel dining room that evening, they did not eat very much.

"Just as I thought," Mrs. Midas said. "I knew they must be tired."

3

Early the next morning—another perfect, sunny Australian winter day—they all got up and had breakfast together outside, on the patio. Everyone was in a good mood.

Mr. and Mrs. Midas were wearing new sunglasses. John and Mary were dressed in their Alice Springs T-shirts, white shorts, and red-white-and-blue jogging shoes.

"We also bought sunhats," Mrs. Midas

said. "The desert sun is very strong. We mustn't get sunstroke."

"We're well equipped," Mr. Midas said. "We're like explorers. Almost. Australians used to travel through the Outback desert on camels. We won't do that, though there are still plenty of camels about. Camels go too slow, and our time is limited."

John sighed. He wished his mother and father would not keep saying their time was limited. He wished nobody had ever invented clocks and watches.

"Thank goodness we're not riding camels!" Mrs. Midas exclaimed. "I've read that they have horrible breath, and the way they walk makes you feel seasick."

"Anyway, the Range Rover's here," Mr. Midas said. "We're going the easy way."

"Is it four-wheel drive?" John asked. He was interested in mechanical details of that sort. It was.

"What color is it?" Mary wanted to know. It was the color of sand.

Mrs. Midas said, "We're going to see the Alice Springs Telegraph Historical Reserve."

"Oh, Mom! *Must* we?" John groaned. He was impatient to begin their expedition to Ayers Rock.

"It's very historic, isn't it?" Mary said, siding with adult authority against him, as usual.

"Let's get going," Mr. Midas said, putting an end to the discussion.

He drove them through the clean streets of the small modern town, with its sprinkled lawns, flower gardens, and brightly painted new bungalows, and onward, about two miles north, to the site of the original settlement. All that remained were several single-story, gray-stone buildings. Mrs. Midas insisted that they enter all of them.

"This was an important telegraph sta-

tion in 1872," she informed her family. "That was the year the telegraph line was completed, linking South Australia with Darwin, the capital of the Northern Territory, and with Britain." Mrs. Midas got the facts from a guidebook, which reminded John of the most boring lessons in school. He liked a lot of things about school, but when it was boring it was the most boring place in the world.

Mr. Midas used only one roll of film at

the telegraph station, so John knew that his father, too, wanted to get on the road.

By ten o'clock they were on their way.

Out on the Stuart Highway, heading south, John felt a bit disappointed. The view was blank—a straight road, the red-brown dust of the desert, a few scruffy, gray shrubs, and the vast blue sky.

"Why would anyone want to live around here?" he asked. "There isn't anything to see."

"That's what some people like about it," said Mr. Midas, who usually worked five days a week in a busy office. "The wide open spaces! No traffic, no crowds! Freedom and fresh air! It's like the Old West, before there was a railroad."

"Are there any Indians?" John asked, sitting up straighter.

"They're called aborigines," Mary said in her superior way. "They've lived here for thousands of years, haven't they, Daddy?"

"Yes, I think so," Mr. Midas said rather doubtfully, because he had forgotten many of the things he had learned in school long ago.

"The aborigines have lived here for forty thousand years," Mary said. "They're the oldest race *anywhere*."

"All right, smarty-pants," John said.

"That's *very* interesting, Mary," Mrs. Midas said. "If John paid more attention to his schoolwork . . ."

"This is supposed to be a vacation," John said.

"Look!" Mr. Midas said, pointing in the direction of a grove of desert oak trees. "I think I saw a kangaroo."

They all looked. They could not see a kangaroo, but they were glad Mr. Midas had changed the subject.

The fat tires whizzed smoothly along the highway. The land was flat. The distant horizon looked as if it had been drawn with a ruler and it never seemed to

get any nearer. They just went on and on.

At a crossroads called Eridunda, which was little more than a name in small letters on the map, they drank some cold apple juice at a roadside café. Then Mr. Midas turned west, along a narrower highway. John felt that now they might be beginning to get somewhere, but the countryside still looked the same. He squirmed beside Mary on the backseat.

"The trouble with this Outback," he said, "is that it's just a big nothing."

After another uneventful hour and a half, they came to a gas station at Curtin Springs and had ham-and-cheese sandwiches and sodas. Then they drove on.

"We'll soon reach Uluru National Park," Mr. Midas said encouragingly.

John yawned.

4

The manager of the Bunyip Motel, near Ayers Rock, was a friendly, fat man with a red face and a yellow beard. When the Midas family arrived, he was standing behind the registration desk in the lobby, with his smile partly hidden by a gray-blue cloud of cigar smoke.

"Welcome to Uluru," he said. "Mr. Midas? Let me see—Midas, Midas, Midas. Yes. We have two nice double rooms ready

for you. Just sign here. My name's Ernie Giles. Call me Ernie."

He was like a tape recorder, full of information, which he recited as Mr. Midas checked in.

"Uluru is the aboriginal name for Ayers Rock," Ernie explained. "It means 'a place of shade and peace.' It is the most ancient, sacred shrine of the Pitjantjatjara Tribe. They worship it as the home of their first ancestors and the spirits that created them. Yakunytjatjara territory is close by. These are difficult names to say and more difficult to remember, even for Australians. There's a guidebook, which helps. Ayers Rock is a huge lump of sandstone, five hundred million years old. It rises one thousand, one hundred and forty feet straight up above the desert. When the world was first formed, the rock was surrounded by sea, which is now very far away. As the sun crosses the sky, the rock seems to change colors—purple, red, orange, and pale brown, and then orange, red, and purple again. It's a beautiful sight. People watch it for hours, and artists come from all over the world to paint pictures of it. If you're going to climb to the top of the rock, I advise you to do your climbing early in the morning, soon after daybreak, before the sun gets too hot."

"Is the climb very dangerous?" Mrs. Midas asked.

"Not really," Ernie said, "as long as you stay on the path. It's clearly marked with a painted white line. And there's a chain you can hold onto at the beginning, the steepest part of the climb. Everyone agrees that the view from the top is worth the effort." He thoughtfully patted the roundness of his belly. "I used to climb the rock when I was younger."

"I'm interested in the aborigines' art," Mrs. Midas said.

"Oh, *Mother!*" John exclaimed. "We saw plenty of art in Sydney!"

Mrs. Midas ignored the interruption, and Mr. Midas raised a warning finger to his lips. "Where are the famous cave paintings?" Mrs. Midas asked.

"You must be referring to the Dream-time paintings!" Ernie said. "Yes, they *are* interesting. Nobody has been able to decide exactly when they were painted, but we think some of them must be thousands of years old, probably the oldest works of art in the world. The aborigines painted pictures on the walls of their caves to make a record, like our Bible, to show what they believed about the making of the world at the beginning of time, and the creation of the seas and lakes and rivers and plants and all living creatures. Sometimes they painted strange spirits that came to their land to help them gather food and protect them against some of the unfriendly forces of nature. There are paintings of religious ceremonies, fights, and dances. Some of the paintings are difficult to understand, perhaps because the ancient paints have faded and have been repainted, with the addition of later stories. Scholars spend years studying all the details.''

After his long speech, Ernie cleared his throat and smiled. "Anyway," he concluded, "in the morning I'll get someone to show you the way to the ranger's office. He has some brochures, and he will introduce you to one of the Pitjantjatjara elders who can guide you to the paintings. He'll charge a small fee, but without help you might have difficulty finding them.''

On the way to their rooms, John said, "Can't we climb to the top of the rock?''

"We'll see," Mrs. Midas said.

John frowned as if in pain and turned to his father. "You said this was going to be an adventure," John said.

"The cave paintings will be *fascinating*," Mrs. Midas said.

"Think how pleased Miss Plimsole will

be!" Mary told John. "When you go back to school, you can write about the paintings—'What I Saw in Australia during My Christmas Vacation.' "

Mary was teasing, as usual, but John was in no mood for a joke.

"Oh, shut up!" he snapped.

"John!" Mrs. Midas said. "Don't talk to your sister like that! As a matter of fact, she has made an excellent suggestion. I'm sure Miss Plimsole would be delighted."

John scrunched his face up tight, like a clenched fist. When Mary was sure that her parents were not looking, she tapped John on the shoulder to attract his attention and daintily stuck out the tip of her tongue.

5

Ranger Musgrave, who was in charge of Uluru National Park, was sitting in his office with a mug of coffee and a thick book when the Midases called on him the next morning. He put down his book and took off his glasses and seemed pleased to tell them about Uluru and its two hundred native inhabitants.

"Dreamtime is what the aborigines call the time when the world was made,"

Musgrave said. "They believe that before Dreamtime there was only dark, empty space. They say Dreamtime is different from ordinary time. It is what our time comes from. Dreamtime's the time that *everything* comes from. You can't measure Dreamtime. It's too big. And it goes around in a circle, like a snake with its tail in its mouth."

Seeing his visitors' puzzled expressions, he added, "I don't understand it either. But that's the strange thing about time: nobody understands it. Time is a very slippery subject. You think that now is now—that should be simple enough. But it keeps getting away from you, doesn't it?" He held out his hands in a gesture of helplessness. "As soon as you try to grab hold of now it turns into then."

Thoughts swam about in different directions in John's head, like goldfish in a bowl. For a moment, he felt quite dizzy.

"I know what you mean," Mr. Midas said to the ranger. "It's almost always later than I think."

"Mr. Musgrave, did you get our message about a guide?" Mrs. Midas asked.

"Yes. You're lucky. Bill Ngoru will take care of you. He knows all about the Dreamtime cave paintings—at least as much as anyone does. If you don't understand the Pitjantjatjara language, he'll speak English. He should be here any minute. Ah! Here he comes."

Mr. Ngoru looked like an old boxer. His brown face was deeply wrinkled around dark brown eyes. His brown hair was yellow in streaks, bleached by all the years' hot sunshine. His red Uluru T-shirt and faded blue jeans bulged with muscles. When introductions were made, John felt that his own fingers were small and were being squeezed smaller in Ngoru's big, powerful hand. The man had a kind smile though.

Mr. Midas followed Bill Ngoru's directions and parked close to the towering brown cliff of Ayers Rock. They walked the rest of the way, past small, crooked trees and dusty bushes, to the caves.

"Here," Ngoru said, pointing to some pale red, gray, and yellow marks on the rough wall of rock beside an entrance deep in shadow. "Dreamtime painting."

"What's it supposed to be?" John asked.

"Quiet!" Mrs. Midas ordered, as if her son had talked during an important speech at school.

"Well, what *is* it supposed to be?" Mr. Midas asked.

"I can see people dancing," Mary said. "Look, there! Aren't they, Mr. Ngoru?"

The old man nodded agreeably.

"Yes," he said. "I can see them, too. Very good."

He led them to the next cave, the next wall painting. It looked very much like the first one. There were short lines that went up and down and long lines that went from side to side. Here and there, lines led to blobs.

"Is that red thing a fire?" asked Mrs. Midas.

Ngoru looked closely at a shapeless red stain.

"That's right," he said, nodding encouragingly.

"I think it looks like a lump of meat," John said.

"Yes," said Ngoru, "it does."

"But which is it?" Mr. Midas demanded. "Fire or meat?"

"It is fire *and* meat," Ngoru said politely. "For Mrs. Midas it is fire. For John it is meat. Dreamtime paintings mean different things to different people. You must decide for yourself."

"What did the people who painted them want them to mean?" Mr. Midas asked.

"I'm sorry, but I cannot tell you what

was in the minds of those people. I know only what is in my mind. You can make meanings for yourself. Then the Dream-time paintings will be your paintings."

John wished they had gone climbing. Walking so slowly and standing still so much made him feel restlessly impatient. He wanted to *do* something.

"What's inside the caves?" he asked Mr. Ngoru.

"You must not go inside," the man said sternly. "Inside is secret. Our tribe strictly forbids visitors to enter our private places. I cannot tell you more than that."

So, of course, the next time the guide, Mrs. Midas, and Mary were studying an old painted squiggle and Mr. Midas was busy taking pictures, John quietly left them and hurried into a cave.

6

As John walked farther into the cave it became narrower and lower and dimmer— light gray, medium gray, dark gray. Soon the ceiling was so low that he had to bow his head. He was in a small tunnel, which suddenly twisted to the left. When he turned the corner, he found himself in total darkness, as black as the middle of a moonless night. The air was cool and damp.

John became aware of the sound of heavy breathing. He looked nervously over his shoulder, but, of course, he could not see anything. He stood still to listen. The breathing was his own. He could feel his heart beating like a tiny drum inside his chest. He tried to whistle, to prove to himself that he was not frightened, but air came out of his pursed lips without any tune.

He raised his hands straight out in front of him and turned around to go back the way he had come. He walked slowly, cautiously, with short steps. His hands touched the rock wall. He must have reached the sudden bend, he thought, so he turned right, feeling his way along the wall. But then he came to another sharp turn to the left. He could not remember having made two turns on the way in, but he kept going, touching the wall carefully with the tips of his fingers.

John wondered why the way back

seemed so much longer than the way in. He opened his eyes wide, trying to see through the blackness.

The tunnel zigged and zagged so many times that he lost his sense of direction. He had an uncomfortable feeling that there must have been a fork in the tunnel and that he had taken the wrong way. He must have walked deep into the heart of the mountain. He considered turning back again but then wondered if he shouldn't just keep going forward and hope for the best.

"Daddy?" he said. "Daddy!" he shouted, and an echo came back to him, *"Daddy!"* "Mommy!" he shouted louder. The echo shouted, *"Mommy!"* "I'm here!" he shouted. *"Here!"* shouted the echo. Then there was a heavy silence.

John was beginning to experience a fluttering, twitchy feeling that was very much like panic when he came to another kink in the tunnel, and there, straight ahead, was brilliant daylight.

"Thank goodness!" he said, stumbling over the uneven dirt floor in his eagerness to get out.

But where were his family and Mr. Ngoru? For that matter, where were the crooked trees and the small bushes? Now there was nothing but desert, just broken rocks and sand. John realized that he must have come into Ayers Rock through one cave and come out through another.

At first, he felt a sense of achievement. Thousands of tourists climbed to the top of the rock every year, but how many, he thought, ever walked through it? He imagined Mary looking around and wondering where he had gone. How mysterious his disappearance must seem to her. He laughed at the idea. But then he remembered his father mentioning that the distance around the rock was more than five miles. He had a lot of walking to do. Which way should he go? The desert landscape was the same whichever way he looked.

He was still trying to decide on his best route back to the motel when he heard a pitiful whimpering, like the plaint of a sad puppy. The sounds were coming from behind a large boulder not far from where he stood. He went to see what was wrong.

A large gray-brown kangaroo was standing beside the boulder. She had a joey, a baby kangaroo, in her pouch. Its little head and two forelegs were sticking out. It was looking up at its mother and mewling. It seemed afraid. She, too, seemed worried. She kept anxiously turning her head, as if expecting trouble from behind. Then John saw what she must be dreading: in the distance, several aborigines were heading her way. They were brandishing long spears.

To his surprise, John found himself speaking to the kangaroo in her own language.

"Why don't you get going?" he said. "They're getting close."

"It's no use," the kangaroo said. "I can't escape. I've come miles and they won't give up. I don't really mind for myself. I've had a good life. But my poor joey . . ."

"You can shake them off easily!" John said. "I'm sure you can! Kangaroos can travel much faster than people."

"I wish I shared your optimism," she said.

"Try!" he urged her. "And hurry! They'll soon get here."

The kangaroo sighed unhappily, patted her joey gently on the head, and moved off, slowly shuffling over the soft sand.

John easily caught up with her.

"Not like that!" he protested. "Put some pep into it! Jump!"

He could hear the hunters' excited shouts, still faint but rapidly loudening.

"*Jump,* for goodness sake!" he said.

The kangaroo paused and looked at him with her eyebrows raised in bewilderment.

"What do you mean, 'jump'? What's that?"

By now John had gotten used to the idea of having met a kangaroo he could talk with; however, he was now astonished to have met one that apparently did not know that kangaroos were designed to

be the best jumpers in the world. Sometimes animals, like people, do not realize
how many useful and enjoyable things
they are naturally capable of doing. They
have to be taught. John hoped there was
time to teach her. He ran and jumped and
ran and jumped and stopped.

"Something like that," he told her,
panting after his exertion. "But you can
do it much higher and longer and faster.
With back legs like yours, you should be
able to leave those men flat-footed."

"There's no harm in trying, I suppose,"
the kangaroo said doubtfully.

"Kick the ground away!" John urged
her. "*Kick!* Again and again! That's the
way!"

Every leap was bigger than the one before. The joey waved goodbye with a smile
on its face, before sinking out of sight into
the safety of its mother's pouch. The kangaroo picked up speed and more speed,
and appeared as only a dark speck, bound-

ing away in a distant cloud of dust, when the aborigines, howling with disappointment, skidded to a halt where she had been.

"Tough luck, you guys!" John said, speaking fluent Pitjantjatjara with a perfect Uluru accent.

7

The aboriginal hunters looked terrible—
sweaty, dusty, droopy, and depressed.
They were wearing so few clothes that
John felt overdressed in his Alice Springs
T-shirt and shorts.

The biggest hunter, scowling angrily,
suddenly lunged at John, seizing his neck
in strong fingers.

" 'Tough luck, you guys!'? Is that all
you can say?" He shook John until the

boy felt that his eyes would pop out.

"I'm sorry!" John spluttered desperately, trying without success to pull the fingers away from his aching throat. He feared he would soon be choked to death.

"He's young," a smaller hunter pointed out soothingly. "He probably cannot imagine how we feel."

"You're right," the big man agreed, roughly putting John down and releasing him. John cautiously felt the bruises on both sides of his neck and nervously swallowed.

"I really am very sorry," John said humbly. "I didn't mean any harm. I'm sure you must be disappointed."

"Disappointed!" exclaimed one of the hunters. "That's putting it mildly. We've been on the go all morning. Twenty miles for nothing!" he complained, impatiently shaking his spear.

Another of them, who was empty-handed, said: "That's the fifth spear

I've lost this week."

"What are we going to tell the women this time?" whined a third, anxiously biting his fingernails.

"They'll be disgusted," the last hunter predicted, frowning. "No meat for dinner again! Oh, dear. I've used up all the excuses I can think of."

John knew about the difficulty of making excuses. Although he was pleased that he had helped the kangaroo and her joey escape being killed, he sympathized with the hunters, too. They also wanted to live. He now noticed that they were badly underweight: their ribs stuck out and their necks and arms and legs were scrawny. In fact, they looked as if they were starving. Life must be hard when you have to catch your food, instead of buying it in a supermarket, John thought.

"It wasn't your fault," he told the hunters consolingly. "That kangaroo was much too fast for you. Nobody could run as fast as she could jump. From now on, you should try stealth. Instead of running after animals and hooting and hollering, you should quietly sneak up on them, until you're close enough to get in some good shots."

They looked at him in thoughtful silence. For a fearful instant, he thought perhaps the hunters in desperation might be considering him for their dinner. He was relieved when a man spoke and his voice seemed friendly.

"Who are you?" he asked.

"John. John Midas."

"Welcome, John. I am Woolara. These are some of my fellow tribesmen—Roowala, Loorawa, and Bamaloodja-dooreeloo."

The hunter with the longest name was the shortest man.

"You can call me Bam, if you like," he said with a shy smile.

"Where are you from, John?" asked

Woolara. "You speak like a Pitjantjatjara, but you don't look like one."

"You are pale," Bam said. "You are covered with strange skins. Have you been sick?" He seemed sympathetic, as if he knew what it was like to be sick.

"I'm fine, thanks," John said, rather doubtfully. "But I'm not quite sure where I am. Please, would you tell me the way to the Bunyip Motel?"

"The Bunyip Motel?" repeated Roowala. "Never heard of such a place."

"It isn't very far from here," John said, though he was not at all sure how far. "It's just on the other side of the mountain."

Woolara shook his head solemnly.

"Nothing is on the other side of Uluru," he said. "You must be mistaken."

John's forehead wrinkled in a frown.

"You look as if you feel mistaken," Woolara added.

"We all sometimes make mistakes," Bam gently pointed out.

"You'd better come back with us," Woolara said. "The women always find *something* to eat. There probably won't be much, but you can share whatever there is."

John looked over his shoulder at the entrance to the cave. He didn't much like the idea of venturing alone into the mysterious darkness.

"All right," he said. "I mean, thanks a lot. I *am* kind of hungry, and it'll be a long walk back to the others."

"The desert's a long place," Loorawa gloomily agreed. "And very wide."

8

They walked and walked and walked and walked. John had never before walked so far. The aborigines might be starving but they were still very good walkers.

The hot sunshine burned John's skin and dried his mouth. He began to feel dizzy with the heat and the steady, silent march across the flat, dusty plain.

Nobody spoke for what seemed to be several hours.

"Is it much farther?" he asked in a hoarse croak.

"Many snakes more," Bam replied.

"How far is that?"

Bam said nothing, only extended his hands as far apart as they would go.

John looked behind now and then to see how far they had traveled. Ayers Rock—Uluru—seemed smaller and smaller as it became more distant. It looked finally like a pebble on the horizon, and then he could not see it at all.

At last, as he was beginning to stumble with fatigue, he heard a faint cry of welcome from a clump of bushes and twisted trees ahead. As bushes and trees cannot grow without water, John hoped they must be approaching a spring.

"Almost home!" exclaimed Woolara, encouragingly patting John on the back. "Soon we shall drink water, and perhaps eat food."

John feebly licked his lips, but his

tongue was so parched that it did not remove any of the dust; his dusty, warm lips made his tongue even drier. The inside of his mouth felt as if it was made of wool. He felt weak with thirst and hunger. Inside his hollow tummy, a tiny, spiraling rumble appealed for help. He imagined drinking a huge, ice-cold soda and eating a whole, enormous pizza with melted cheese and sliced tomatoes and olives and anchovies on it, and then drinking another huge soda, and then . . .

He was about to decide what sort of ice cream he wanted most of all, when he felt a small hand clutch his left leg below the knee. He looked down. A small boy with big, brown eyes looked up at him.

"Is there some meat?" the boy asked.

"No, we didn't bring any," John said. "I'm sorry."

"Oh."

Big tears filled and overflowed the boy's eyes, trickled down his brown cheeks, plopped onto the hot desert sand and immediately disappeared.

Women and children gathered around the hunters. There were moans of disappointment and a few harsh words of complaint.

"Nothing?" one of the women asked Loorawa. "What happened to your spear *this* time?"

He shrugged his shoulders and stuck out his lower lip in an embarrassed way.

"I threw it too soon, too far," he explained miserably. "The kangaroo dodged and ran away. I couldn't find the spear. I wanted to go on searching, but the others said they couldn't wait."

"Loorawa!" the woman cried. "You promised!"

"I did my best, Rujee," he said. "We ran all the way to Uluru. You've never seen such a kangaroo. When we thought it had given up trying to escape, it suddenly seemed to fly!"

"We had bad luck," Bam told a woman who was much bigger than himself. "Forgive us, Ulka. I pray you did better than we did."

"We women fortunately do not depend on luck," Ulka said. "We have been busy with stones and pointed sticks all day. We collected a few things." She noticed John and raised her black eyebrows in surprise. She lowered her head and hissed into Bam's ear. "We have hardly enough for ourselves. You brought a *guest*?"

"It's traditional desert hospitality," Bam uncomfortably reminded her. "We found him near Uluru. He was lost." Bam raised his voice. "John, come and meet the rest of the tribe."

The big, red sun was beginning to set when John followed the hunters and their families into the shade of the oasis, where the temperature was only 97 degrees. Trying to make the best of a bad situation, the women brought the men spring water in thick, gray cups made of sun-baked mud. The water was cool. After only a few gulps, John felt better. He looked forward eagerly to eating.

The men sat in a circle on the ground under the trees, and the women and children sat in a group nearby. John did not have to wait long.

"Here you are, John," Ulka said, offering, between her finger and thumb, a fat grub, about two inches long, whose many legs were wiggling in a frenzy to get away.

He stared at it in horror and his lower jaw fell open. He made no attempt to take the squirming creature from her.

"Go on," she said. "It's all right. There's really plenty for all of us."

"What's *that*?" he asked.

"A witchetty grub, of course. Don't be bashful. Any friend of Bam's is always welcome."

"You expect me to *eat* it?" he said.

"Well, I know it isn't kangaroo," she

said irritably. "I was hoping we'd have a kangaroo feast tonight. But witchetty grubs are very nutritious. Don't they eat witchetties where you camp?"

"It's alive!" he protested. He could feel his innards tightening in disgust.

"Certainly it's alive," she said. "I dug it out from under a log just this afternoon. It's a nice, big, juicy one."

Bam, who had been refilling John's cup, came back from the spring and realized something was wrong. John turned to him.

"Don't you think this—this thing—would be better cooked, Bam?"

John had read about people in France who eat snails and frogs' legs and say they are delicious. Maybe witchetty grubs would not seem so bad once they stopped wiggling and twitching about.

" 'Cooked'?" Bam said.

"Yes. Grilled, perhaps. Or baked or fried. Cooked any way."

"What *is* he talking about?" Ulka demanded. The day had been a long, hard one; she was not in any mood to have a long discussion with this unexpected, ungrateful visitor, who apparently thought he knew more about how to serve witchetties than she did. "Here," she said to Bam, "you take it. I'm busy." She went away, leaving Bam holding the frantic grub.

"Do you like eating them?" John asked. Bam looked around to make sure nobody else was listening before he answered.

"If you don't tell anyone, I'll tell you a secret," he said in a low voice. "I *hate* them! When you bite them, they squish in your mouth."

"How can you do it?"

Bam looked around again and spoke in an even lower voice.

"I usually throw mine away and only pretend I've eaten them. I don't even like lizard. Most days, unless I'm dying of hunger, I just eat berries and leaves and things like that."

"That's not much, is it?" John said.

"No, it isn't. That's why I'm little."

John felt very sorry for him.

"You might enjoy the grubs if they were cooked," John said. "Would you like me to try cooking a couple? I can grill them over a fire."

Bam looked baffled.

" 'Fire'?" he said. "What's that?"

John laughed. Bam must be kidding.

"Seriously. Where's the fireplace?" John asked.

But there was no fireplace, and no fire.

John realized that if he wanted to eat cooked witchetty grubs, then he would have to show them how to make a fire.

9

"Fire makes heat and light, like the sun," John told Bam. "Fire makes many kinds of food taste better, and it's good for heating water with, when you want a hot bath. Fire's nice to sit around at night, when the sky is dark and the air is cold. Fire is useful, and I think you'll like it."

"But what is it?" Bam asked.

"It's hard to describe. The best thing would be to show you. I'll make some."

John hoped he would be able to. He remembered the time when an Eagle Scout had demonstrated Indian-style fire-making at cub-scout summer camp. John's troop had cheated a bit on their test, using a cigarette lighter to get their fire started. But John understood the way you were *supposed* to make fire without matches. So his mother had been allowed to sew a fire-making merit badge onto his cub-scout uniform.

"I'll *try* to make some," he said now.

"I'd better tell Woolara," Bam said. "He always likes to know what's going on. He's our leading hunter."

John did his best to explain to Woolara what fire is and what it's for. Woolara was very interested.

"If you want us to help with the magic by singing and dancing," he said, "you'll have to teach us the words and music. We haven't ever done this before."

"Thank you," John said, "but singing

and dancing won't be necessary. What I need is a thick piece of softwood, a stick of hardwood, and some wood chips or grass and leaves and twigs."

Woolara looked puzzled but nodded politely and ordered some of the younger men to gather everything John had asked for. After a brief search, they were able to cut the required materials with their stone knives.

John sharpened one end of the stick and made a small hole in a log. He laid the log on the stony ground in a clearing and fitted the point of the stick down into it. He placed the palms of his hands on opposite sides of the stick. He moved his hands vigorously to and fro, so that they twirled the stick, one way and then the other, again and again.

The aborigines—men, women, and children—crouched close around John and gazed intently at the stick as it revolved, back and forth, faster and faster, in the log. They were expecting something marvelous to happen, but they did not know what. John looked around at the dark heads against the dusky blue sky of twilight. They seemed to have faith in him and he wished he would succeed.

"Is this fire?" Bam asked uncertainly.

"Not yet," John said. "You'll know when it happens."

There was just enough daylight for John to see the first thin wisp of smoke rising from the log, where the friction was heating it.

"Watch!" he said. "It should begin any moment now!"

He twirled the stick even more briskly, and the gray smoke thickened. The onlookers wrinkled their noses, opening their nostrils wide and sniffing the unfamiliar smell.

"Ah!" John exclaimed triumphantly, as he saw the first pale yellow flicker of flame. "Quick, Bam! Put grass and twigs around the place where the stick and the log come together. But gently!"

Bam did as he was instructed, while John kept working hard with the stick.

Suddenly the flame leaped up, spreading through the kindling.

"*Aie!*" exclaimed the watchers, for they could see that the magic had started.

"More, Bam! More!" John shouted.

Bam eagerly piled on the twigs.

"Put on some of the bigger ones!" John said. "Then small sticks and big sticks!"

As fuel was added, the flames multiplied and climbed higher. The wood crackled. Orange sparks flew upward in the darkening blue of the evening.

"*Aie! Aie! Aie!*" cried the excited watchers, raising their arms and backing away from the glow and the heat.

John felt proud. "If you can find a few more of those witchetty grubs," he said, "I'll show you how you can cook them."

"It is now nighttime," Ulka pointed out. "The witchetties live among the bushes, where it is dark until the morning. Is it possible to make fire in the day?"

"Any time," John assured her. "But we needn't wait until tomorrow. At night, you can see by the light of a fire. That's one of the good things about it. Look."

He picked up the safe end of a long, burning stick and held it above his head. The flickering flame revealed the nearer branches of trees, which cast long, flickering shadows.

"Show me the way to the witchetties' hiding places," he said. "You'll be able to get some grubs now."

Witchetty-hunting by torchlight was a new experience that made some of the women giggle with excitement. They soon dug out half a dozen grubs, then a dozen, then more.

"We'll have to wait a little," John said, when they were all seated once more around the fire. "At cub-scout camp we used to roast potatoes in the red embers, when the fire was almost finished. Let's sit here and wait till it's just right for cooking. This is the time for singing," he suggested to Woolara.

The aborigines had not understood everything John said, but they got the general idea, and they were so pleased by the fire's appearance that they sang some of their happiest, loudest songs. They woke up a platypus sleeping in a pool nearly a hundred yards away.

When the hot ashes were ready, John showed them how to stick green wooden skewers into the witchetties—after they had been killed, of course, as quickly as possible.

He cooked the grubs for only a short time. The smell of roasting witchetties was like the smell of roasting turkey and reminded John of how hungry he was. There were general murmurs of pleasure, curiosity, and impatience. "When are we going to have a taste?" was a question asked more than once.

When the witchetties were as brown as barbecued spareribs, he removed the grubs one by one, while holding up a hand like a traffic cop to try to keep everyone away from them until they were cool enough to eat.

Roowala was so eager that he ignored the warning. He reached past John and grabbed a witchetty, and immediately dropped it on the ground.

"Ouch!" he yelped. "It bit me!"

"The heat burned you," John explained. "Fire can be dangerous." But the aborigines were in no mood for a lesson on the dangers of fire. They were clamoring for the cooked grubs.

The grubs were shared and soon eaten.

"The crisp bits are delicious!" said Ulka, who now seemed much friendlier toward John than when he and the other hunters had first got back to the oasis.

"I like the soft centers, too," Bam said.

"I know it's late," Woolara said to Ulka, "but I'm sure we'd all appreciate another batch, if you women feel up to the task."

John put some more fuel on the fire and quickly revived it, then lit another long torch and led a second, willing expedition into the witchetty bushes. This time the search took a little longer, but they eventually brought back more than two dozen grubs, including several that John thought could be called jumbo size.

When he had finished licking his fingers, Woolara made a short, formal speech.

"I believe I am speaking for all of us," he said, "when I say that John has conferred upon us a great and wonderful gift that we shall always be grateful for."

A few people applauded, but most of them were already fast asleep, gently snoring, lying down where they had been sitting, in the last, faint red glow of a small heap of charcoal.

10

When the rising sun awoke John the next morning, he thought anxiously about his family. Even Mary must be worried about him. He wondered whether his father was searching the desert by Range Rover. Would he be able to drive where there were no roads? How could he possibly know which way to go? John looked around in all directions from the oasis and saw absolutely nothing out there in the early heat-haze except miles and miles of dusty, gray-brown rock and parched, red-brown earth—a vast, flat emptiness. He was glad he was not alone.

"Is anything wrong?" Bam asked him.

"Oh, no," John said bravely. He knew the truth might well hurt Bam's feelings.

"I've brought you some berries and water," Bam said. "They're all we're having for breakfast." His small shoulders rose and fell as he sighed. "Our cooked supper last night was so good that everyone in camp is talking about food even more than usual. We have to go hunting. Although we hardly ever catch anything but a sleepy old lizard now and then, the women insist that we keep trying. They say we can't sit around eating witchetty grubs all day. Soon there'd be none left; they're getting scarcer here every day. Do you want to come along? You don't have to if you don't want to. I wouldn't blame you if you don't."

"Of course, I'll do anything I can," John promised, doing his best to smile. "Not that I know much about hunting," he admitted. He almost added, "Except what I've seen on TV," but he realized that Bam probably didn't know what television was, either, and it would be difficult to explain.

"Maybe today we'll get lucky," Bam said, not very convincingly.

When John walked to the pool to get some water to wash with, he encountered Loorawa, the hunter who had already lost five spears that week. The aborigine was sitting on a rock near the trees, trimming a straight branch he had just cut to make a sixth.

"Frankly," Loorawa said, uneasily frowning, "I'm afraid this is a waste of time and wood. It would be better to use it making fire. Fire uses up wood, but at least you're sure of getting something for your trouble."

"I have an idea that may solve your problem," John said. "You don't seem to have any boomerangs, do you?"

As John had expected, Loorawa had not heard of Australia's most famous weapon. "I'm having enough trouble with spears," he said gloomily.

"Boomerangs are much better," John said, realizing as he spoke that he sounded like a commercial for boomerangs. "They go faster and farther. If they hit what you're trying to hit, they hit harder. And, if they miss, they come back to you, so you can try again."

"You're not joking, are you?" Loorawa asked suspiciously, because the other hunters sometimes teased him about all the spears he lost.

"I'm telling the truth," John said. "If you can find the right piece of wood, I'll show you how to carve it right now."

With a twig, John drew the curved L shape of a boomerang full size in a smooth patch of sand. Loorawa, with all his spear-making experience, was a highly skilled carpenter who was able to work quickly. As soon as he saw what was needed, he went immediately to the right hardwood tree to cut off a matching curved L-shaped section of branch. Under John's direction, he carved the rough wood so that its upper surface was smoothly rounded, its lower surface was smoothly flat, and its forward edge was as smoothly sharp as a knife.

John explained how Loorawa had to hold the boomerang by the tip of its longer blade in his right hand and to throw it in such a way that it would spin around and around on its way to the target—"like a propeller," John said, "like a sycamore seed, I mean." Loorawa did not know what he meant by propellers or sycamore seeds, but John said it didn't matter; the important thing was to throw the boomerang properly, and, if necessary, to keep

throwing it until Loorawa hit what he had to hit.

The other hunters were in no hurry to get started on another day's hard walk in the hot sunshine. John had plenty of time to take Loorawa into the desert at the edge of the oasis, as far as possible from the pool and the palm-frond shelters, to teach him how to throw his boomerang. John was not an expert on throwing boomerangs, but since he had seen a short movie about them, he was an expert compared with Loorawa.

John stuck Loorawa's unfinished new spear into the ground as a target and showed the hunter how to aim the boomerang at it.

With Loorawa's first few tries, either the boomerang did not go far enough, or it went too far, or else it went to the left or to the right of the target. But each time it turned and spun back to him, and Loorawa was able to catch it without moving more than a few steps one way or another. When he managed to hit the branch, John moved it farther away, until the hunter was usually able to hit it at a distance of about fifty yards, half the length of a football field.

"Great!" John exclaimed, and Loorawa looked pleased.

At that moment, a boy near John's age rushed out from between the trees.

"Loorawa!" he shouted. "Woolara's calling you. I've been looking all over. Come on!"

"All right, all right," Loorawa said with a worried frown.

"Why are you so late?" Woolara asked Loorawa when he and John joined the small group of hunters. "The women are nagging again. Haven't you made a new spear?"

"I haven't finished it," Loorawa said. "I'm taking this instead." He held up the strange, new-fangled gadget and shook it. "It's a boomerang."

"It looks silly to me," Woolara said. "It hasn't even got a point."

"Please don't blame Loorawa," John said. "It's my fault he's late. I showed him how to make a boomerang."

Woolara was too polite to complain to a guest, but John could see that the leader did not think much of the boomerang's appearance. John heard him muttering to himself: " 'Boomerang'! What a silly name! My father always used spears, and spears are good enough for me. . . ." He raised his voice. "Well, come on then. Let's go. Hasn't anyone made you a spear, John? Bam, you should have helped him."

Bam looked embarrassed.

"It's all right, thank you," John said. "I'll just come along to advise Loorawa."

Woolara's eyes rolled upward in astonishment.

"A hunter with an adviser instead of a spear!" he said. "We'd better go before the women find out what's going on. They'd think we were crazy!"

The four aborigines set off. John followed.

"Wait a minute!" he said. "May I make a suggestion?"

"What is it?" Woolara asked as patiently as possible, while the group waited.

"Wouldn't it be better to walk that way?" John asked, pointing in the opposite direction.

"We always go this way," Woolara said.

"But this is the way the wind is blowing," John said. "If we go this way, the wind will carry our scent ahead of us and warn all the animals we're coming. They won't get that warning if we go against the wind, and we'll have a much better chance of catching them by surprise."

"I never thought of that," Woolara honestly admitted. Though he was a strict leader of his tribe, he was willing to consider advice from a stranger. John's cooking lesson had made a very favorable impression.

"All right, John," Woolara said. "We'll try it your way."

So they turned to face the light eddies of hot, dusty wind.

They had walked for almost two hours and John was already beginning to feel a bit dizzy with the heat when Bam halted them with an urgent, loud whisper: "Look! Kangaroos!"

There were four of them, big ones. They were only about a hundred yards away, but they were hard to see, because they were as gray as the scruffy thorn bushes they were feeding on, as gray as the semicircle of boulders that shaded them from the fierce white sun.

"Get ready!" said Woolara eagerly.

"Hold it!" said John, with a cautious hand on Woolara's arm. "Let's not run in a bunch or they'll get away!"

"Then what *should* we do?" Woolara asked, trying not to sound annoyed.

"Give Loorawa and me time to work our way around to behind the boulders. Then, when we wave, you lead the others straight ahead, making as much noise as you can. You'll drive them into our ambush."

"An ambush without spears?" Woolara objected doubtfully.

"An ambush with a *boomerang*," John pointed out. "Please let us try."

"Well, we couldn't do much worse than we have been doing," Woolara admitted. "All right, we'll try it your way."

So that was the agreed plan.

As soon as Loorawa and John reached their hiding places behind two of the bigger boulders at the far end of the semi-circle, Woolara and the others charged across the open desert, shouting and screaming terrible threats and brandishing their spears.

The kangaroos looked up in alarm, turned, and bounded away. As they passed close to the boulders, John nudged Loorawa and said: "Now! Pick a male! Throw for his head!"

Loorawa's throw was wild. The boomerang missed its target by several feet. But it swiftly flew back to him and he caught it.

"Really *aim*, Loorawa!" John urged him.

The hunter concentrated hard. He threw the boomerang with all his strength—just in time, before the fourth kangaroo, a fully grown male, could jump out of range.

The sharp edge of the boomerang hit the side of the kangaroo's head with such great force that he immediately fell dead. He could not have felt a thing.

On the homeward march, Loorawa was allowed the honor of carrying the kangaroo. The body was a heavy burden, which made Loorawa's shoulders and back ache, but he beamed with pride all the way. John carried the boomerang.

"You are a very good adviser," Woolara graciously told him.

The rest of the tribe greeted the triumphant hunters with loud cheers.

That evening there was a splendid banquet. By the end of it, the children's full bellies were as round as balloons, and so were some of the grown-ups', especially Bam's. Afterward, there were speeches and songs, which were much appreciated by those who were still awake.

11

There was a bustle of activity in the camp the next day. All the men and older boys were busy cutting timber, carving boomerangs, and learning how to throw them.

A great deal of wood had been burnt in the big, long-lasting fires of the past two nights, and most of the best trees were now being reduced to stumps. The second-best trees did not bear many branches suitable for boomerangs.

At one point, a young man began to cut one of these few remaining branches and another pulled him away from it. "That branch is mine!" he shouted. "Get away from it!"

"What do you mean it's yours?" the first man angrily demanded, threateningly raising his sharp stone knife. "I saw it first!"

"But you've already made two boomerangs. I've been collecting wood for the fire."

"That's your problem."

One word led to another. Soon they were fighting. Fortunately, the stone knife was dropped after the first punch. The two men rolled around on the sand, hitting each other, twisting each other's arms and legs, until . . .

"Stop!"

The loud, commanding voice of Woolara brought them to their feet.

"Look at you two!" the chief said in

tones of withering contempt. "One black eye and one bleeding nose. I wonder how they are going to help us."

The two men bowed their heads in shame.

Woolara ordered them to apologize to each other and shake hands. Meekly, they did so. Then Woolara announced that there must be an emergency meeting of the entire tribe, men, women, and children.

When they were all gathered together, with John standing to one side at the back, Woolara climbed on top of a convenient rock and solemnly addressed them.

"We of the Pitjantjatjara Tribe are, above all, lovers of peace," he said. "We believe in sharing everything—our happiness and our troubles.

"We are lucky. Our guest, John, has brought us fabulous magic from the other side of Uluru—fire, which has put within our power the heat and the light of the

sun, and the boomerang, the-weapon-which-comes-back, which can improve beyond measure our chances of enjoying plenty to eat. These are important benefits. We are grateful."

He nodded in John's direction. The boy modestly lowered his eyes and blushed with pleasure.

"But as our lives become richer and more complicated," Woolara sternly went on, "we must never forget that we are still equal members of one tribe. We all know what it is like to be hungry, even starving. Suddenly we have been blessed. But the blessings will be worth less than nothing if we cannot share them in peace. Let us hear no voices raised in selfish anger. And let no man ever fight against his neighbors."

There was a general murmur of agreement and some applause. Woolara raised a hand to restore silence.

"This morning's eager search for wood for boomerangs," he said, "has made me realize that the time has come, a little sooner than usual, to move camp. We have to give the trees of this oasis a chance to grow again, the grubs a chance to multiply. Land and its creatures sometimes need rest. We have to go on to fresh abundance. Let us have a quiet evening. We will leave tomorrow at dawn."

12

Uluru appeared on the horizon after the tribe had been walking for about four hours. When John first saw the mountain it seemed tiny, but it gradually grew during the long, hot day.

Seeing such a familiar landmark made John even more miserable than the tiresome, dusty trek had. He missed his family—and he missed the comforts of family life. He thought of his father's strength and his mother's gentleness. He thought of hot water hissing from a modern shower, clean clothes on the shelves of his bedroom closet, delicious meals at the family table. He thought he would really like to watch television with Mary. He might even let her choose the program. He wondered whether he would ever see his family again. After all this time, they might even have given him up for dead and gone home without him. His eyes became watery and he sniffed.

The sun was already low and their shadows stretched far across the desert in front of them when Bam, who had the sharpest eyesight, spotted the oasis. "Palm trees!" he cried, as relieved as a sailing ship's lookout spying land at the end of an ocean voyage.

They arrived in the blue dusk of early evening. It was still light enough to see that the new oasis was much larger and more luxuriant than the one they had left behind.

"Look at all the gum trees, dear!" Rujee exclaimed to Loorawa. "Plenty of wood for boomerangs!"

"Plenty of witchetty grubs!" her husband replied. "Plenty of wood for fire to cook them with!"

Inside a dense stand of trees, John came to the edge of a pool, a pond almost as big as a lake, and heard the continuous burble and soft roar of a waterfall. He stooped, cupped his hands, and drank cool water until he could drink no more. It was delicious.

Woolara did not take much time to look around. "We'll sleep here tonight," he said, indicating some soft grass that was sheltered on three sides by bushes and trees. "We'll make our camp after we've had a good night's sleep."

Everyone gratefully agreed. They were

all exhausted. Soon the fine, star-lit night was abuzz with snores.

John was more than half asleep when he heard a strange, prolonged hiss, like steam from a radiator. But he was too tired to wonder what it might be.

13

The aborigines were in very good spirits when the sun woke them the following morning.

An adventurous little girl found a second big, deep pool, hidden in a grove of bamboo. She reported the pool to Woolara, who inspected it and decided it would be good for bathing in, while the other would provide their drinking water.

The bathing pool was popular. Long

after they had washed the desert sand from their hair and the dust and sweat from their bodies, many of the tribespeople stayed in the pool, splashing each other, swimming, or quietly floating on their backs. Bam was a good swimmer who liked showing off by diving under the water and coming to the surface where the more timid bathers least expected him.

John worked hard, collecting weeds, twigs, and small branches for a cooking fire.

Some of the women were grinding flour from wild grain in earthenware bowls. In the past, they had mixed water with flour to make dough and had simply dried it on hot stones in the sun. John had told them about something called "bread," and now, when the fire was ready, they were going to try to cook some.

John went back beyond the bushes to collect more fuel so he could build a good fire for baking. While he was looking for some small logs, he encountered Bam's wife, Ulka, crouching, digging with a pointed stick.

"Any luck?" he asked cheerfully.

Ulka scowled.

"Not one witchetty," she said. "The ground is hard."

"Why don't you poke the stick into one of these cracks and hammer it in with a rock?" John suggested. "Then, if you wiggle the stick around, maybe you could open up a deep hole. Then, maybe—"

"All right," she interrupted. "I was digging for witchetty grubs before you were born."

"Sorry," he mumbled. "I just thought . . ."

In spite of her angry tone, she did what he had suggested, and very soon she was able to split a chunk of earth loose. When she pulled it out of the ground, she also brought out several shiny blue pebbles of a kind that John had never seen before.

The smallest of them was the size of a pea, the largest the size of a walnut. The most extraordinary thing about them was their coloring: they were as blue as the Australian sky, with strange, milky depths and tiny glints of green and red. They were beautiful.

"Ulka!" he exclaimed. "I think you've found a jewel mine!"

"I don't know what you're talking about," she said.

"Those stones! I bet they're worth a lot," John said.

Ulka wrinkled her nose as if she had noticed a bad smell. "Take them, John, if you think they're so wonderful. They aren't worth anything to me. We can't eat stones."

John was disappointed by her lack of enthusiasm, but the discovery delighted him. Smiling, he reached down and plucked from the earth a stone of medium size, about the size of an olive, and stuck it into a pocket in his shorts.

There was no time to pick up any more, though, because just then he heard a terrible disturbance coming from the direction of the bathing pool—a splashing, thrashing, crashing noise followed by an explosive hissing and a turmoil of shrill screams.

There was an even louder scream right beside John's ear. Ulka sounded hysterical. The boy jumped a step back from her.

"Aie!" she wailed. "It must be the terrible Rainbow Serpent! These stones you made me dig up must be his treasure! Now he'll eat us all! My mother warned me against the Rainbow Serpent!"

She was obviously too upset to explain any more.

John ran through the camp, grabbing a couple of boomerangs on the way, and hurried as fast as he could to the pool.

There he came upon a frightening sight.

The Rainbow Serpent was the biggest snake he had ever seen, longer and wider than a full-grown palm tree. It was covered with shiny, metallic, multicolored scales, all reflecting the sunlight as from a thousand mirrors.

The serpent was violently squirming about in the pool, making the water overflow with high waves and a white foam of bubbles. One moment the serpent raised its blunt head, with its fiercely swiveling red eyes, its huge jaws, its long, sharp, white teeth, and its long, forked black tongue, to the full extent of its body, reaching up as high as a house. The next moment it plunged down into the water again with a gigantic *splash*. Then up again, sending a glittering cascade in all directions.

Screaming in panic, every man, woman, and child succeeded in scrambling out of the pool and running beyond the monster's reach—except one.

The next time the serpent reared up, John saw it held a small, struggling man between its jaws. John was horrified when he recognized his friend's desperate face.

"Bam!" John shouted.

There was not a second to waste. John aimed and hurled one of the two boomerangs; but, just as it was about to reach its target, the serpent moved its head, and the boomerang harmlessly whistled past. Without waiting for it to return, John threw the second one.

This time, he scored a direct hit on one of the serpent's most tender parts, its big, bulging, red left eye.

There was a sniffling, snuffling, snorting bellow of pain. The serpent's nostrils, like two red tunnels, and its jaws, like the steel claws of an enormous steamshovel, opened wide.

The serpent's tail was furiously churn-

ing the water into a turbulent froth that looked like a storm at sea. But Bam, who had fallen into the pool when the monster opened its mouth, was swimming his fastest, and soon climbed ashore uninjured.

John was sighing with relief when the serpent's angry, red right eye spied him. The monster lowered its head with stunning speed, grabbed the boy around the waist, and lifted him high above the pool.

At first, John was too surprised to be frightened. But then he was very, very frightened indeed, as he felt himself sucked into the serpent's slippery, darkening mouth. He realized that unless he did something right away, he was in danger of being swallowed.

But what could he do?

Sometimes in an emergency the brain comes up with a wonderful idea—too bad if it doesn't. John's brain had never before had to think so quickly, so well.

Moving swiftly, John seized the two

long points of the serpent's divided tongue. They were wet but rough, like a cat's tongue, so he was able to get a firm grip. Remembering one of the most secure knots that he had learned as a scout (a triple running-bowline-sheep-shank, which is impossible to undo, unless you know how), he tied together the two sections of tongue, yanking them as tight as he could.

The effect was remarkable. The serpent's shrieking, howling roar sounded like the combined noises of a hurricane and an earthquake.

Like Bam, John was dropped immediately into the pool. And like Bam, John got out of the water without delay.

The serpent twisted and turned, trying in vain to get away from itself and the pain in its mouth. If it had not just threatened John and his friends, he might have felt sorry for it. He didn't.

As the serpent thrashed to and fro more

and more frenziedly, it stirred up so much spray that it made a fine, brilliant haze between the oasis and the blue sky.

And then this giant creature of many colors, in a final, terrible, dying convulsion, leaped high up into the sunshine and formed a great curve that looked just like a rainbow.

14

The serpent had disappeared and the camp was safe again.

A group of hunters with boomerangs hurried out into the desert and returned with a kangaroo for a big celebration.

This was the happiest occasion of all.

Long after the children had been sent to their soft beds of fragrant leaves to count the stars of the Southern Cross until they fell asleep, the men and women sat around the last glowing coals, singing the many verses of a new song about the great discoveries and achievements of the past few days.

As their eyelids began to feel pleasantly heavy, members of the tribe retired one by one. Only a few remained when John got to his feet and gave Woolara his thanks and said goodnight.

"We thank *you*, John," Woolara said. "We will always be grateful."

"You saved my life," Bam said.

"I'm glad I was able to help," John murmured modestly.

"You are a hero and a beloved friend," Woolara said. "I hereby name you a Lord of the Pitjantjatjara. It's a very rare honor, because I just thought of it."

"Thanks a lot," John said. "I really appreciate that."

"But there must be something else that we can do to show our gratitude," Bam suggested.

"Yes," Woolara agreed generously. "If there's anything you can think of, John, just say the word. If it's anything within my power, it's yours."

John thoughtfully bit his lower lip for a moment. "Well," he said hesitantly, "there is one thing."

"What is it, John?" Woolara asked.

"I've been very happy living with the tribe," John said, "but I miss my mother and father terribly." After a brief pause, he added, "I even miss my sister. I'd be very grateful if you'd help me get back through Uluru so I can find them. I just hope it's not already too late."

"We cannot possibly take you *through* Uluru," Woolara said rather nervously. "We never go into the caves. The caves are very strictly taboo. Nobody who has entered them has ever returned."

"I came through before," John said. "I must try to go back. If I don't, I'll never see my family again."

"You are a brave boy," Woolara said. "We will help you as much as we can. We will take you to the place where we found you. Then you will be on your own."

"All right," John said. "On my own."

In the faint, pink glow of the dying fire, he could not be sure but he thought he saw the gleam of tears in the leader's eyes.

15

The next day, there was much affec-
tionate backslapping and hugging as John
said farewell. The whole tribe wanted the
honor of escorting John back to Uluru,
but the leader ruled that the trip would be
made best by only the four hunters who
had found John there. Woolara himself
led the way.

Even after he and his escorts had left
the oasis far behind, John saw men,

women, and children continuing to wave to wish him a good journey.

Finally, they reached the towering brown cliff of Uluru.

"It's so big!" John said anxiously. "It all looks the same. How will we ever find the right place?"

"Don't worry, John," Bam said, patting him on the back.

But John could not help worrying.

Woolara smiled, and said, "We of the Pitjantjatjara Tribe will always remember The Place of the Jumping Kangaroo, where we first met you. We will tell our children The Story of John Midas, and our children will tell their children, for ever and ever."

That would be nice, John thought. Even so, the great, vertical rock face looked impenetrably mysterious. He dreaded the thought of getting lost inside the dark maze of the mountain.

"Here you are, John," Woolara said.

"Good luck and good hunting, wherever you go."

John gulped and timidly waved good-bye, then resolutely turned to face whatever he had to face.

As he walked farther into the cave it became narrower and lower and dimmer—light gray, medium gray, dark gray. Soon the ceiling was so low that he had to bow his head. He was in a small tunnel. When it suddenly twisted, he found himself in total darkness, as black as the middle of a moonless night.

Now he didn't know where he was or which way he was going and he wondered whether he had been wise to leave the protection of his friends. Perhaps he was heading for the secret lairs of awful monsters. But he felt he had to go on. He walked steadily, with his hands outstretched in front of him.

After many zigs and an equal number of zags, the blackness suddenly turned into dark gray, medium gray, and light gray, and then he saw a glimmer of daylight ahead.

And then, with a deep breath, he walked out once again into bright sunshine.

16

"Oh, *there* you are, John!" said Mr. Midas. "I wish you'd stay put. I want you in this picture, too. Stand between Mary and Mr. Ngoru."

"You really should pay closer attention to what Mr. Ngoru's telling us," Mrs. Midas said. "Having come so many thousands of miles, we shouldn't waste this wonderful opportunity to learn about the culture of the aborigines."

"This painting," the guide said, pointing to the rock face, "shows the Rainbow Serpent. This huge snake was one of the most feared creatures of the Dreamtime. It could be found in any waterhole, swamp, or lake. If anyone disturbed it, the Rainbow Serpent might eat him or her alive. But always at last it would leap from the water and rise into the sky as a rainbow. Here you see . . ."

John took a close look at the faded, old painting.

"That looks like the one with the bruised eye and knotted tongue!" he exclaimed.

Mr. Ngoru looked surprised.

"So you have been reading a book of our Dreamtime stories," he said. "That's one of our favorites, the one about the Boomerang Hero who saves the tribe. It was he who taught us how to make fire."

"I know," John said.

"Don't be silly!" Mary protested.

He leaned closer to the painting.

"But I do. I was there. Look!"

He pointed a finger at a crude splotch of white paint beside splotches of black paint beneath the great arc of a rainbow.

"That's me!" he said.

"Pooh!" Mary retorted scornfully. "That's the Boomerang Hero."

"I was the one who taught them how to make boomerangs. Can't you see my Alice Springs T-shirt? That's me after I threw the boomerang into the Rainbow Serpent's eye and tied his tongue into a knot. I . . ."

"Why do you always try to turn everything into a silly joke?" Mary demanded.

"Now, children!" Mrs. Midas said. "Mr. Ngoru is telling you all about the old legend. It's rude to squabble when he's talking."

John was beginning to have doubts. What had really happened? At the oasis, his T-shirt and shorts had been wrinkled and travel stained. Now they were like new.

"Look this way, you guys!" Mr. Midas said, peering through his camera. "That's it. Smile!"

John was amazed. He had been away for days—no, thousands of years!—yet apparently he had been away for only a few seconds. Had he imagined everything?

As he obediently posed for the camera, he put his hand into the pocket of his shorts and felt his beautiful blue stone. That was no imaginary myth. That was real. He *had* really traveled into the Dreamtime.

John knew something about gems and thought he knew what it was—a valuable opal. He could hardly wait to have the stone wrapped as a gift, to give to his mother at the Bunyip Motel tomorrow, on

Christmas morning. He smiled at the thought of the expression on Mary's face then.

The ranger of Uluru National Park was right. As he had said, "Time is a very slippery subject."

ALICE SPRINGS - AHAKISTA

ABOUT THE AUTHOR

Born in London, *Patrick Skene Catling* was educated there and at Oberlin College in the United States. As a Royal Canadian Air Force navigator and as a journalist, he has traveled extensively. His present home is in the Republic of Ireland.

The original appearance of his best-selling fantasy, *The Chocolate Touch,* in 1952 stirred much reviewer enthusiasm. *The New York Herald Tribune* remarked, "it has already proved a hilarious success with children," and *The Saturday Review* said, "it is told with an engaging humor that boys and girls will instantly discover and approve."

ABOUT THE ILLUSTRATOR

Jean Jenkins Loewer studied at the University of Buffalo and, after earning her degree there, did graduate work at Hunter College in New York City and at Marywood College in Scranton, Pennsylvania. She has taught art at all levels from elementary grades to college, as well as adult education classes. She has illustrated several children's books, including three titles in Andre Norton and Dorothy Madlee's *Star Ka'at* science fiction series and *Today's Special: Z.A.P. & Zoe.* She lives in the Catskill Mountains in Sullivan County, New York.